3

Bear Child's Book of Hours

Anne Rockwell

Thomas Y. Crowell New York

Library of Congress Cataloging-in-Publication Data
Rockwell, Anne F.
    Bear Child's book of hours.

    Summary: For each hour of the day Bear Child
participates in a new activity, and as he does the
reader sees the time on the clock.
    [Time—Fiction. 2. Bears—Fiction] I. Title.
PZ7.R5943Bf 1987   [E]   86-24245
ISBN 0-694-00196-1
ISBN 0-690-04551-4 (lib. bdg.)

Good morning!

It is eight o'clock
in the morning.

Bear Child is getting dressed.

It is nine o'clock.

Bear Child is eating breakfast.

It is ten o'clock.

Bear Child is helping do the dishes.

It is eleven o'clock.

Bear Child is playing in the park.

It is twelve o'clock.

Bear Child is shopping for lunch.

It is one o'clock.

Bear Child is eating lunch.

It is two o'clock.

Bear Child is working in the garden.

It is three o'clock.

Bear Child is playing with a neighbor.

It is four o'clock.

Bear Child is building with blocks.

It is five o'clock.

Bear Child is taking a bath.

It is six o'clock.

Bear Child is eating supper.

It is seven o'clock.

Bear Child is listening to a story.

Now it is eight o'clock
at night.

Bear Child is going to bed.

All night long
the clock hands are turning
while Bear Child is sleeping.

Then eight o'clock
in the morning comes again.